The Bush

by Bernard Ashley
illustrated by Lynne Willey

Tamarind

Tamarind Ltd

For Luke, Rosie, Carl and Paul

Published by Tamarind Ltd, 2003
PO Box 52
Northwood
Middx HA6 1UN
UK

Text © Bernard Ashley
Illustrations © Lynne Willey
Edited by Simona Sideri

ISBN 1 870516 60 5

Printed in Singapore

Joyce danced when the rabbits came.

There was a 'he' buck rabbit and a 'she' doe rabbit.

They weren't at all like the thin, grey rabbits Joyce saw in the open country they called the bush.

These were fat, white rabbits with pink eyes and fluffed up fur. They were bigger and a different shape.

Joyce's mother bundled them out of her basket and put them together in one wooden hutch.

A week later, Mum put each rabbit in a hutch on its own. She said to Joyce's two older brothers, "Get some wood and make more hutches, please."

"What for? Two's enough, isn't it?" said Joyce.

"Come on, boys," said Mum. "Joyce, you're just getting in the way there. Let the boys get to work. Think about it, what happens when you put a buck rabbit and a doe together in a hutch? That'll tell you why we need more than two hutches for these rabbits!"

Joyce soon found out why they needed more hutches.
A month later, the doe had six babies, all pink and bald.

They all looked the same, even when they grew fur.
Joyce liked all the rabbits, but there was one special one
that was more cuddly than the rest.

At feeding time, Joyce called out, "Rabbit! Rabbit! Rabbit!
Rabbit! Rabbit!" One after the other, five rabbits scurried out,
pink eyes blinking, to feed on the green plants that
Joyce held out.

Then, when her special cuddly one appeared, Joyce called out,
"Kipenzi!" which means 'favourite'.

"Are the rabbits for us to play with?" Joyce asked her brothers.
But they didn't know.

That night, as she stroked and fed Kipenzi, Joyce asked her mother. "Are these rabbits our pets?"

"No, Joyce," replied her mother. "When they're full grown, they're going to The Bush. Then I get paid. This way we earn money."

This seemed good to Joyce – all the rabbits growing strong and then being let loose in the open country, free in the bush.

"That's good," she said. But she couldn't understand why her mother would get paid for it.

Joyce's little sisters fed the rabbits too, but they didn't care for any of them. Her brothers didn't care either. Joyce did.

Every time Joyce went to his hutch, Kipenzi would come out and sit on her lap while she stroked him gently.

When they had eaten all their food, the other rabbits hopped away, but Kipenzi seemed to want to be a friend. He licked Joyce's fingers and nibbled at her skirt.

"Don't get too fond of that thing," Joyce's mother said. "Remember, he's going to The Bush."

Joyce dreaded the day she would have to let Kipenzi go, hopping off into the open country. But at least he'd be hopping off to freedom.

Joyce counted the days. At first it was next week when Kipenzi would have his freedom. Then it was tomorrow, now it was today!

Joyce cuddled Kipenzi and tried not to cry.

Her mother put the rabbits into six separate sacks. Joyce left her hand in Kipenzi's sack till the string trapped it so tight she had to give a big tug to get it free.

Joyce and her mother left the father and mother rabbit behind. They carried the six young rabbits in their sacks to wait for the bus at the side of the road.

Joyce made sure she was the one holding Kipenzi's sack. She wasn't letting go of him till they got to the open country, to the bush.

Then the bus came.

But where was it going? It didn't take them
along the hard mud track towards the open country.
It took them along the big road to the city.

"This isn't the right way to the bush, is it?"
Joyce asked her mother.

But her mother wouldn't answer any questions.

When they arrived in the city her mother started asking questions. She asked directions.

She had four sacks of wriggling rabbits and Joyce had two sacks.

Her mother was asking, "Where's The Bush? Can you show me the way to The Bush?"

A woman told her, "Along this road…"

Joyce couldn't understand what was happening.
The open country was nowhere near where they were walking.
The streets were full of people. There were shops and
cars and bikes and buses. They were going on and on
to where the buildings went higher and higher.
The tops of them looked as if they were going
to touch like fingertips.

Then suddenly Joyce found out where they were going!

There, in red writing on the front of a big building were words she could read clearly. 'The' and 'Bush'…

The bush wasn't the open country bush at all. The Bush was the name of a big hotel.

Joyce stopped. "Is this where we've been heading?"

Her mother nodded.

"This is it. Round at the back, to the kitchen."

"*The kitchen?*" Joyce hugged Kipenzi's sack to her chest.

Kitchens meant cooking pots and pots meant things going into them.

Like rabbits. Like Kipenzi.

"He's going to be killed! For eating!" Joyce almost screamed it at her mother.

"Yes, for eating. That's what we get paid for."

Now Joyce *did* scream. "Not Kipenzi. Please, not Kipenzi!"

"Joyce! Stop that noise! Now come on." Joyce's mother led the way round to the yard at the back of the hotel, which was next to a golf course.

A man was sitting in the yard, outside the back door.

Past him, Joyce could see inside the kitchen. There were long, sharp knives hanging from racks, steaming pots and bubbling pans. The man stood up. He was very tall and looked quite fierce.

"Rabbits," said Joyce's mother.

"How many you got?"

"Six."

"Give." He thrust out his hand and grabbed the four sacks that Joyce's mother was holding. The man scowled down into each of the sacks. He pulled out one rabbit for a closer look. He handled it so roughly it made hurt sounds. "They all the same?"

"Yes."

The man's fierce look said that they'd better be the same. He pulled the other three rabbits out and crammed all four into one sack. "Two more?" he clicked his fingers.

"Here they are." Joyce's mother took one of the two sacks from Joyce and gave it to him.

"That's five," he growled, cramming this rabbit into the sack too.

Joyce's mother was looking at Joyce. "Give that to the man!"

But Joyce was gripping tight onto Kipenzi's sack. The butcher wasn't having Kipenzi. "No! No! Not Kipenzi. Take five."

"I want all six!" said the man and grabbed the sack.
In a second, Kipenzi was crammed in with the rest.

"There's no need to be so rough!" said Joyce's mother.

"I'll get your money," said the butcher.

He set the bulging rabbit sack on his chair, swung around and headed into the kitchen.

Joyce was suddenly at the chair. She grabbed the bag and tipped out all the rabbits. "Go! Go!" she shouted.

She used her foot to send the rabbits scuttling across the yard and through the fence to the golf course.

"What are you doing?" her mother shouted, trying to round up all the rabbits and catching none.

The butcher was trying to catch them, too. His big hands grabbed about, but a scared rabbit is too fast for a butcher any day. "Come back here!" he shouted. "Come back. Come back here!"

But one rabbit *was* still back there.
Kipenzi. He was tame so he hadn't run away.
He was sitting big-eyed on the chair,
waiting to be stroked.

Joyce and her mother and the butcher
all seemed to see him at the same moment.

Three pairs of hands came grabbing at him.
Joyce's for love, the butcher's for the knife, and
Joyce's mother's for... what?

They found out because she was the winner.

Joyce's mother got there first. She grabbed Kipenzi and held him in her arms.

The butcher looked at her. Joyce looked at her. What was she going to do with Kipenzi?

The butcher said, "Give!"

Joyce shouted, "Don't!"

Kipenzi stayed calm and Joyce's mother said, "Sorry,"
over her shoulder and took Joyce and Kipenzi out of the yard.

Mum strode back to the bus park to get the bus home.
She spoke not one word all the way – even when
she gave Kipenzi to Joyce to hold. She looked straight ahead,
out through the bus window.

   Joyce said nothing, either, she just cuddled Kipenzi.
But her heart was thumping just as fast as his.

Finally, at the bus stop, when no-one else could hear them and no-one else could see them, Joyce's mother spoke. Not with a shout, but with a slow shake of her head. "It was his rough hands. It was the way he handled those little creatures. He was so cruel. I don't like seeing any animal treated that hard. I'm glad you helped them get away."

Then Mum set off towards home, going in front with a firm step. "We'll just have to earn money some other way. We'll plant and grow."

Joyce followed, smiling and stroking Kipenzi, every step of the way.

OTHER TAMARIND TITLES

The Feather – NEW for 2003
Boots for a Bridesmaid – new edition for 2003
Dizzy's Walk
Zia the Orchestra
Mum's Late
Rainbow House
Starlight
Marty Monster
Jessica
Yohance and the Dinosaurs
Kofi and the Butterflies

FOR OLDER READERS, AGED 9–12
Black Profile Series:
Benjamin Zephaniah
Lord Taylor of Warwick
Dr Samantha Tross
Malorie Blackman
Jim Brathwaite
Baroness Patricia Scotland of Asthal
Chinwe Roy

The Life of Stephen Lawrence

AND FOR YOUNGER CHILDREN
The Best Mum NEW for 2003
The Best Toy NEW for 2003
Are We There Yet? – new edition for 2003
Time for Bed – new edition for 2003
Let's Feed the Ducks
Let's Go to Bed
Let's Have Fun
Let's Go to Playgroup
Where's Gran?
Toyin Fay
Dave and the Tooth Fairy
Kim's Magic Tree
Time to Get Up
Finished Being Four
ABC – I Can Be
I Don't Eat Toothpaste Anymore
Giant Hiccups